Ladybird  Readers

Sleeping Beauty

Series Editor: Sorrel Pitts
Text adapted by Mary Taylor
Activities written by Catrin Morris
Illustrated by Richard Johnson
Song lyrics by Wardour Studios

LADYBIRD BOOKS

UK | USA | Canada | Ireland | Australia
India | New Zealand | South Africa

Ladybird Books is part of the Penguin Random House group of companies
whose addresses can be found at global.penguinrandomhouse.com.
www.penguin.co.uk   www.puffin.co.uk   www.ladybird.co.uk

Penguin
Random House
UK

Text adapted from *Read it yourself: Sleeping Beauty*, first published by Ladybird Books Ltd, 2018
This Ladybird Readers edition published 2021
001

Printed in China

A CIP catalogue record for this book is available from the British Library

ISBN: 978–0–241–47560–7

All correspondence to:
Ladybird Books
Penguin Random House Children's
One Embassy Gardens, 8 Viaduct Gardens, London SW11 7BW

MIX
Paper from
responsible sources
FSC® C018179

Sleeping Beauty

Picture words

the king

the queen

Princess Aurora
(the princess)

good fairy

bad fairy

the prince

cast a spell

spinning wheel

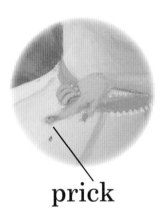

prick

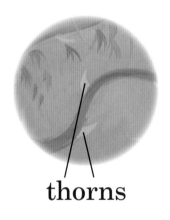

thorns

hedge

soldier

5

The king and queen wanted a baby very much. When they had a baby girl, they were very happy!

"Let's call her Aurora!" said the queen.

"Yes, Aurora! What a lovely name!" said the king.

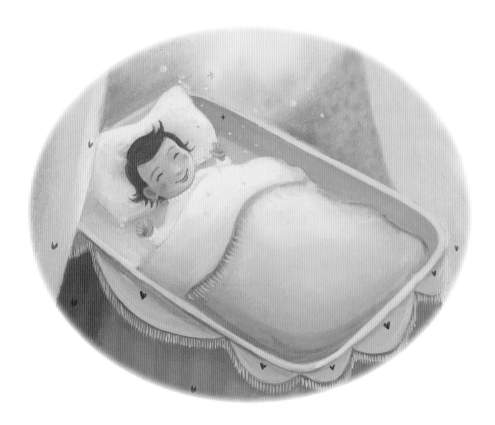

The king and queen invited
the fairies to come and see
the new baby.

"Oh, she's beautiful!" the fairies
said. "Let's cast spells for
baby Aurora!"

While Aurora slept, the fairies cast spells for her.

"Princess Aurora is going to be clever!" said one fairy.

"She is going to love animals, and they are going to love her!" said a second fairy.

At that moment, another
fairy arrived.

It was the bad fairy, who hated
the king and queen!

When the bad fairy arrived, Princess Aurora began to cry.

The bad fairy flew near to her and cast a spell.

"At the age of fifteen, the princess is going to prick her finger on a spinning wheel . . . and she is going to die!" said the bad fairy.

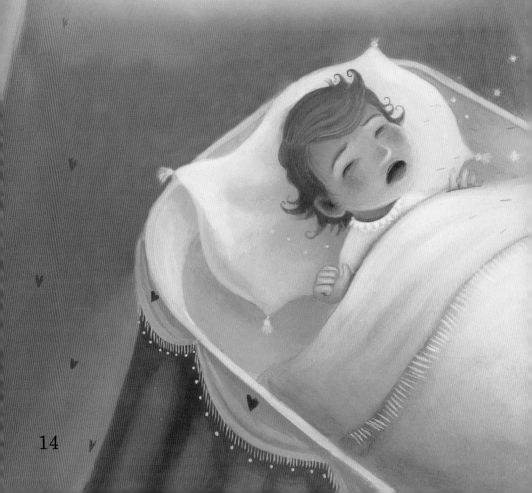

The king and queen and the good fairies were all afraid.

But then, one of the good fairies cast a spell, too.

"I can't *stop* the bad fairy's spell, but I can *change* it! Princess Aurora *is* going to prick her finger on a spinning wheel, but she is *not* going to die! She is going to fall asleep for a hundred years," said the good fairy.

"After a hundred years, the princess
will need to have her family and
friends with her," said another fairy.
"So all the people in the castle will
fall asleep with her, too!"

"I don't want Aurora to prick her finger on a spinning wheel, and I don't want her to fall asleep for a hundred years!" said the king.

"Bring all the spinning wheels in the country here, and break them all!"

People brought their spinning wheels, and the king's soldiers broke all of them.

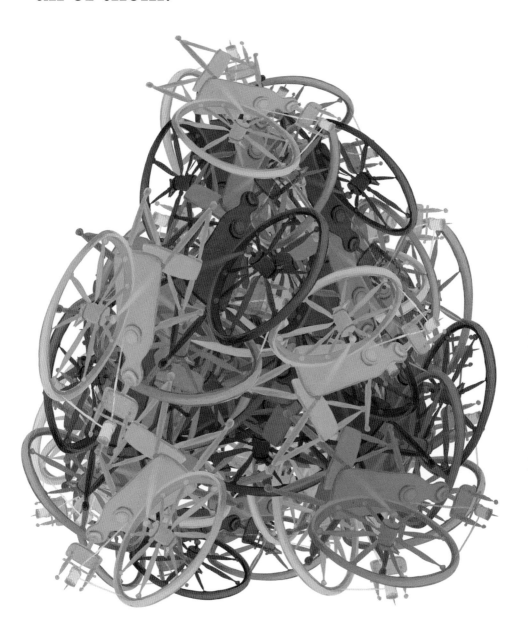

Princess Aurora grew up. When she was fifteen years old, she was a clever, beautiful young woman.

She loved having picnics in the castle's gardens with her animal friends. She was very happy.

One day, the princess found
something in her bedroom.
It was made of wood, and it had a
wheel on it.

"What's this? Where did it come from?" Princess Aurora thought, and she sat down next to it.

Princess Aurora touched the spinning wheel . . . and pricked her finger!

She fell on the bed and was soon asleep.

In other rooms in the castle, people fell asleep.

The king and queen fell asleep where they were sitting.

Some people were eating. They fell asleep at the table.

Soldiers fell asleep while they were standing.

The dog was lying on the floor. It fell asleep, too.

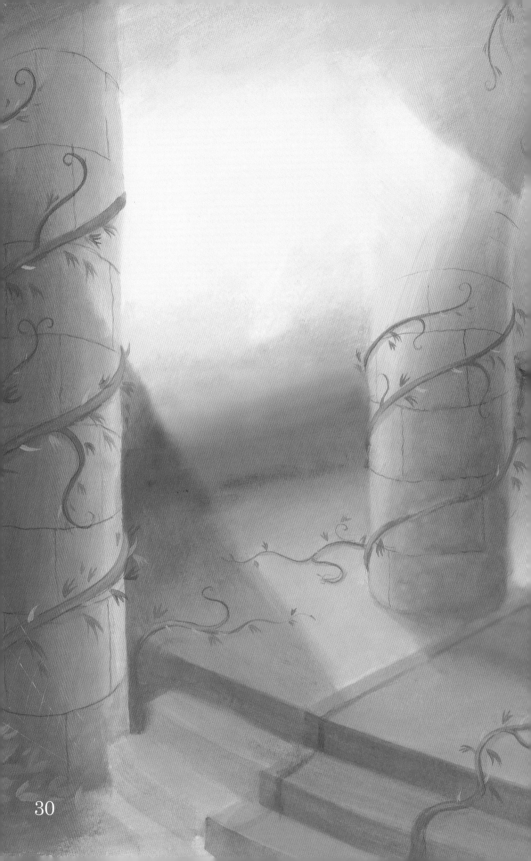

Thorns grew inside the castle in every room.

Outside, a thick hedge of thorns grew around the castle. The thorns were hard and strong.

People couldn't go through the hedge. Soon, they could only see the top of the castle.

Many people forgot there was a princess and her family inside it.

33

The thorns grew for a hundred years. Then, one day, a prince was riding through the country.

A very old man told him the story of the sleeping princess and her family.

The prince decided to go to the castle.

"I'm going to find the princess!" he thought.

The prince cut down the thorns and climbed up the castle's walls.

Through a high window, he saw the princess asleep on her bed.

"What a beautiful girl!" he thought.

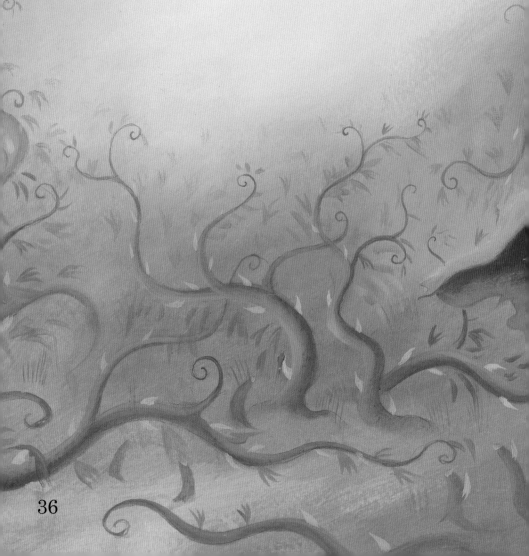

The prince kissed the princess, and she opened her eyes.

Princess Aurora looked at the prince. "Are you a dream?" she said.

"No, I'm not a dream," he said. "I'm a prince, and I'm here to wake you up."

Then, all the people and animals who were sleeping woke up.

The king and queen woke up.

The dog that was lying on
the floor woke up.

The soldiers woke up, too.

"Thank you, young man, for waking us up!" the king said to the prince.

"What can we give you to thank you? Please, tell us," said the queen.

"I would like to stay here with you for a few months," said the prince.

"Of course!" said the king and queen. "We would like that, too!"

The prince and the princess spent a lot of time together.

She began to love him. He began to love her.

Princess Aurora and the
prince got married.

There was a big party
that evening.

The fairies came, too . . .
but the bad fairy
wasn't invited!

Activities

The key below describes the skills practiced in each activity.

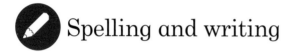 Spelling and writing

Reading

Speaking

Listening*

Critical thinking

Singing*

Preparation for the Cambridge Young Learners exams

*To complete these activities, listen to the audio downloads available at www.ladybirdeducation.co.uk

1 Circle the correct pictures.

1 He is Princess Aurora's father.

 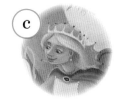

2 She does bad things.

3 This is part of a plant, and it can hurt you.

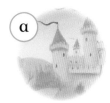 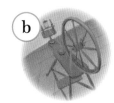 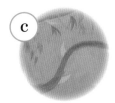

4 He looks after the king and queen.

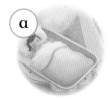 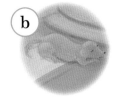 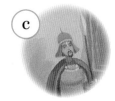

2 Find the words.

p	u	t	w	t	m	a	p	b	s
l	u	f	i	n	g	e	r	a	p
a	c	a	s	t	l	e	i	l	r
y	g	i	b	e	h	n	c	l	i
i	c	r	t	l	r	p	k	l	n
n	x	y	h	p	o	e	e	t	c
h	e	d	g	e	o	y	g	h	e
c	t	b	e	e	m	c	a	o	s
a	w	s	o	l	d	i	e	r	s
r	b	t	a	r	t	m	r	n	w

castle

fairy

finger

hedge

soldier

thorn

prick

princess

3 Ask and answer the questions with a friend. 💬 ❓

1 *Who are the people in the picture?*

The king and queen, their baby, and some fairies.

2 Why did the good fairies visit the baby princess?

3 What spell did the bad fairy cast on Princess Aurora?

4 What happened to Princess Aurora and the people at the castle?

4 **Read the text. Choose the correct words and write them next to 1—5.**

arrived   was   flew   cast   began

When the bad fairy [1] _____arrived_____,

Aurora [2] _____ to cry.

The bad fairy [3] _____ near

to her and [4] _____ a spell.

She said that Aurora [5] _____

going to die.

5 Circle the correct words.

1 While Aurora slept, the fairies cast spells for

a her. **b** him.

2 "The Princess Aurora is . . . to be clever!" said one fairy.

a not going **b** going

3 "She is going to love

a animals!" **b** children!"

4 "And they are going to . . . her!" said a second fairy.

a hate **b** love

6 Read the story.
Choose the right words and write them on the lines. 📖 ✏️ ⬡

1 After	Before	When
2 needs	is needing	will need
3 As	If	So
4 always	too	together

"¹ _____After_____ a hundred years, the

princess ² _____ to have her

family and friends with her," said another

fairy. "³ _____, all the people

in the castle will fall asleep with her,

⁴ _____!"

7 Circle the correct words.

1 Princess Aurora grew **down.** / **up.**

2 She was **fifteen** / **fifty** years old.

3 She was a clever, beautiful
old / **young** woman.

4 She **hated** / **loved** having picnics
in the castle's gardens with her
animal friends.

5 She was very **happy.** / **sad.**

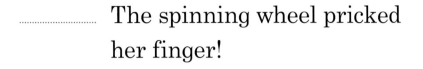
.... The spinning wheel pricked
her finger!

.... She fell on the bed and was
soon asleep.

.... She touched the spinning wheel.

....1.... Aurora found a spinning wheel in
her bedroom.

9 **Read the questions. Write answers using the words in the box.** 📖 ✏️

king and queen   floor   soldiers

1 Who fell asleep where they were sitting?

The king and queen fell asleep where they were sitting.

2 Where was the dog when it fell asleep?

3 Who fell asleep while they were standing?

10 **Write the correct form of the verbs.**

Outside, a thick hedge of thorns
.......grew....... **(grow)** around the
castle. The thorns .... **(be)**
hard and strong. People ....
(cannot) go through the hedge.
Soon, they .... **(can)**
only see the top of the castle. Many
people .... **(forget)** there
.... **(be)** a princess and her
family inside it.

11 Talk with a friend about the pictures. One picture is different. How is it different? ⬤

1

Picture b is different. It is only the prince.

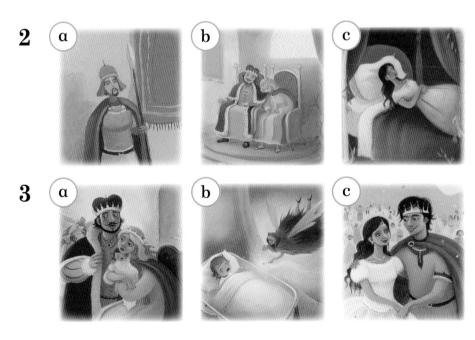

12 **Look and read. Choose the correct words and write them on the lines.** 📖 ✏️ ⭐

> thorns   cast a spell
> prick   spinning wheel

1 The prince cuts them from the castle walls.   _thorns_

2 Aurora hurts her finger on this.   _____

3 Aurora finds this in her room.   _____

4 The bad fairy does this to Aurora.   _____

Listen and color.
Use the colors below.

14 Who said this?

the
queen

the
king

the
prince

the
princess

1 "Let's call her Aurora!"

said .... the queen ....

2 "Are you a dream?"

said ....

3 "Thank you, young man,

for waking us up!"

said ....

4 "I would like to stay here with you,"

said ....

15 Look at the pictures.
Tell the story to your friend. 🗨 ⬤

1

2

3

4

5

6

*A king and queen
had a baby girl
called Aurora . . .*

16 Write about your favorite character in the story. Why is he/she your favorite?

My favorite

17 Sing the song. 🎵

The king and queen had a baby girl
They wanted good things for her
They invited all the fairies to the castle
To come and see their daughter.

Princess Aurora is sleeping now
If you listen carefully, you will learn how
The bad fairy put a spell on her
And she became the Sleeping Beauty.

The bad fairy hated the king and queen
The good fairies could not stop her
She cast a spell on the baby girl
But the good fairies made it better.

Princess Aurora is sleeping now
If you listen carefully, you will learn how
The bad fairy put a spell on her
And she became the Sleeping Beauty.

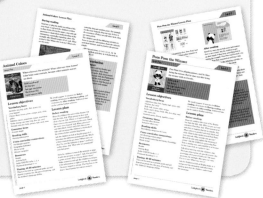